Dinosaurs
DO

Dinosaurs DON'T, Dinosaurs DO

by Steve Björkman

Holiday House / New York

For every kid who accidentally steps
on someone's tail or pokes a friend
with one of his or her horns

I LIKE TO READ is a registered trademark of Holiday House, Inc.

HOLIDAY HOUSE is registered in the U.S. Patent and Trademark Office.
Printed and Bound in March 2012 at Tien Wah Press, Johor Bahru, Johor, Malaysia.
The text typeface is Report School.
The artwork was created with pen and ink and watercolor.
www.holidayhouse.com
3 5 7 9 10 8 6 4 2

Library of Congress Cataloging-in-Publication Data
Björkman, Steve.
Dinosaurs don't, dinosaurs do / by Steve Björkman. — 1st ed.
p. cm. — (I like to read)
ISBN 978-0-8234-2355-2 (hardcover)
1. Etiquette for children and teenagers—Juvenile literature.
I. Title. II. Title: Dinosaurs don't, dinosaurs do.
BJ1857.C5B56 2011
395.1'22—dc22
2010032832

ISBN 978-0-8234-2640-9 (paperback)

GRL E

Dinosaurs
don't do this.

Dinosaurs do this.

Dinosaurs don't run here.

Dinosaurs do run here.

Dinosaurs don't play
like this.

Dinosaurs play like this.

You want red.

Dinosaurs don't
tell others
what to like.

Dinosaurs ask others
what they want.

Grrrrrrr!!!
Help!

Dinosaurs don't hit or bite.
When they are mad,
dinosaurs use words.

Dinosaurs don't eat like this.

Dinosaurs eat like this.

Dinosaurs don’t just take, take, take.

Dinosaurs do share.

Dinosaurs don't use mean words.

Dinosaurs do use nice words.

They don't yell here.
Yahoooo!

They do yell here.

When dinosaurs make a mess,
they don't walk away.

They clean up.

Dinosaurs treat others
as they want to be treated.

That is why everyone loves dinosaurs!